First published in 2018 by Ragged Bears Ltd
Sherborne, DT9 3PH
www.ragged-bears.co.uk

ISBN: 978 1 857144 73 4

A CIP catalogue record for this book is available from the British Library

Printed in Poland using sustainably sourced paper

All Except Winston

Rochelle Brunton
illustrated by Nicoletta Bertelle

Ragged Bears

In the warm African sun, the giraffes stretched up their long necks to reach the sweetest fruit and the highest twigs.

The young giraffes ate
and ate
and ate.

All except Winston
who ate alone.

In the cool shade of the Acacia Tree, the giraffes stretched down their long necks to reach the watering hole.

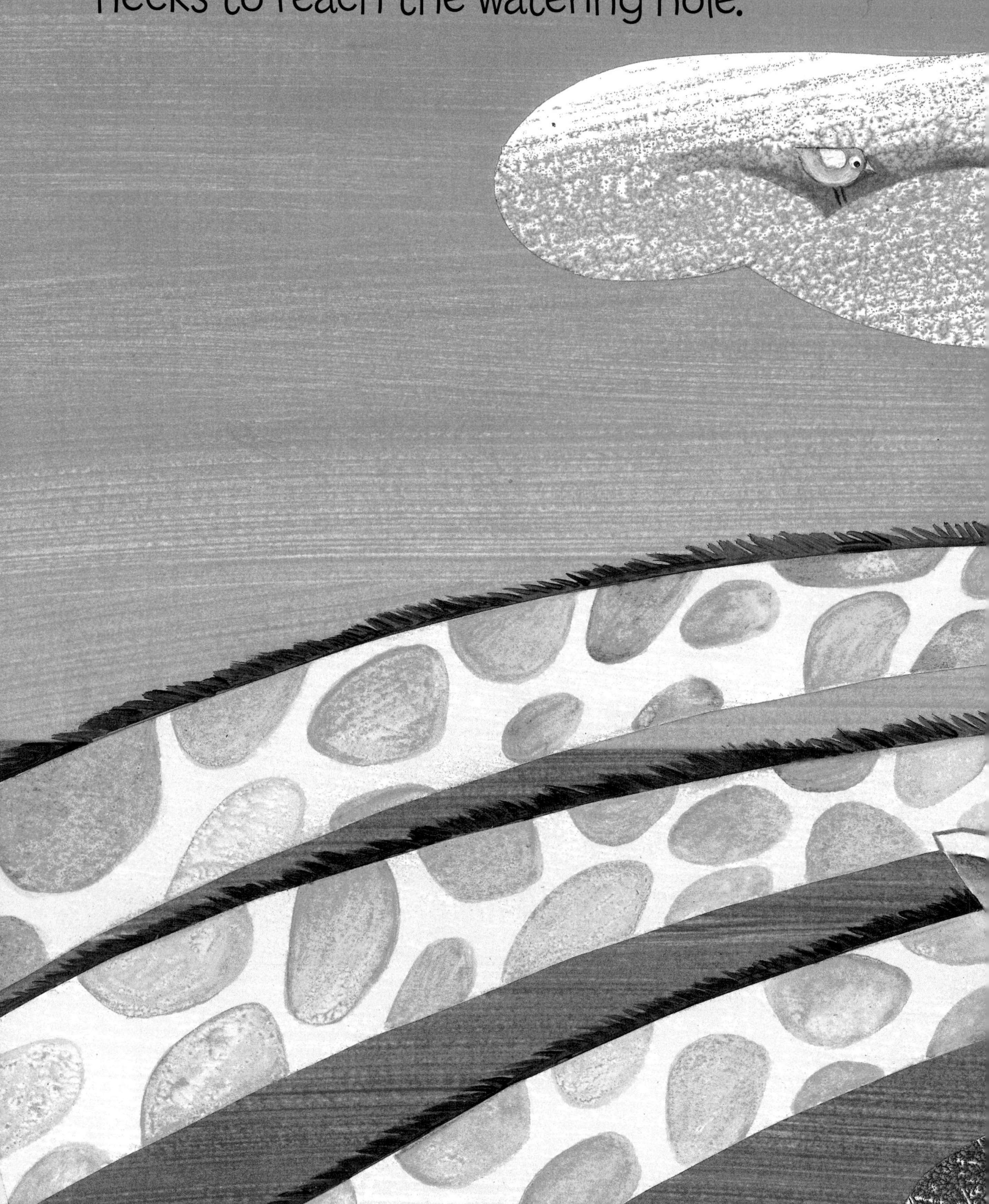

The young giraffes
drank
and drank
and drank.

All except Winston
who drank alone.

In the sweet-smelling grasses of the Savannah, the giraffes stretched out their long necks to play a game of 'who can be the tallest'.

The young giraffes played
and played
and played.

All except Winston
who played alone.

In the darkness of night under the twinkling stars, the giraffes stretched their long necks on the soft grass.

Together, the young giraffes slept
and slept
and slept.

All except Winston
who slept alone.

Then one day whilst the giraffes were enjoying their fruits and twigs high amongst the tree tops, there was a rustle of bushes and a loud 'snap' of twigs.

The giraffes continued to eat and eat and eat.

All except Winston . . .

Jumping to attention, Winston let out a shrill whistle,

'Fweeeeeeeet!'

which startled the birds and caused the monkeys to swing from the trees.

By the time the hungry lion had appeared from behind the shrubs, the giraffes had made a galloping head start.

Winston and the young giraffes ran and ran and ran, through the Savannah . . .

past the Acacia tree and into the dusk, until the lion had disappeared far behind them.

In the bright morning
sky with the sun rising
before them, the giraffes
returned to the Savannah,
tired but safe.

'Three cheers for Winston!'
all the animals cried out.

The young giraffes cheered
and cheered
and cheered.

All except for Winston, who sat proudly on the back of one of his new friends, feeling like the happiest and tallest giraffe in all of Africa.